CLEVER DOG, KIP!

For Elizabeth and Josephine

A Red Fox Book

Published by Random House Children's Books
20 Vauxhall Bridge Road, London SW1V 2SA

A division of Random House UK Ltd
London Melbourne Sydney Auckland
Johannesburg and agencies throughout the world

Copyright © Benedict Blathwayt 1996

1 3 5 7 9 10 8 6 4 2

First published in Great Britain as *Kip, A Dog's Day* by Julia MacRae 1996

Red Fox edition 1999

Printed in China

RANDOM HOUSE UK Limited Reg. No. 954009

ISBN 0 09 926532 X

CLEVER DOG, KIP!

Benedict Blathwayt

Red Fox

Cock-a-doodle-doo

Good morning, Kip.

Let's make a start.

Hurry up, Fudge, I've got a busy day ahead.

Come on, Kip, let's go and fetch those sheep.

These are the best for the Show.

That was close!

Woof! Woof!

Woof! Woof!

Hurry up!
We must get
the bales in.

Kip!

Come here, Kip!

There you are, Kip.

Just in time.

Don't forget the eggs.

Goodnight, Fudge.

Clever dog, Kip.

What a day we've had!

Time for your supper, Kip.

Goodnight, Kip.

Some bestselling Red Fox picture books